Put Beginning Readers on the Right Track with
ALL ABOARD READING™

The All Aboard Reading series is especially designed for beginning readers. Written by noted authors and illustrated in full color, these are books that children really want to read—books to excite their imagination, expand their interests, make them laugh, and support their feelings. With fiction and nonfiction stories that are high interest and curriculum-related, All Aboard Reading books offer something for every young reader. And with four different reading levels, the All Aboard Reading series lets you choose which books are most appropriate for your children and their growing abilities.

Picture Readers
Picture Readers have super-simple texts, with many nouns appearing as rebus pictures. At the end of each book are 24 flash cards—on one side is a rebus picture; on the other side is the written-out word.

Station Stop 1
Station Stop 1 books are best for children who have just begun to read. Simple words and big type make these early reading experiences more comfortable. Picture clues help children to figure out the words on the page. Lots of repetition throughout the text helps children to predict the next word or phrase—an essential step in developing word recognition.

Station Stop 2
Station Stop 2 books are written specifically for children who are reading with help. Short sentences make it easier for early readers to understand what they are reading. Simple plots and simple dialogue help children with reading comprehension.

Station Stop 3
Station Stop 3 books are perfect for children who are reading alone. With longer text and harder words, these books appeal to children who have mastered basic reading skills. More complex stories captivate children who are ready for more challenging books.

In addition to All Aboard Reading books, look for All Aboard Math Readers™ (fiction stories that teach math concepts children are learning in school) and All Aboard Science Readers™ (nonfiction books that explore the most fascinating science topics in age-appropriate language).

All Aboard for happy reading!

To my parents, Bill and Bobbie East,
who always tucked me in at night,
"snug as a bug in a rug"—C.E.D.

To my parents, Ted and Gale Dubowski—M.D.

Text copyright © 1995 by Cathy East Dubowski and Mark Dubowski. All rights reserved.
Published by Grosset & Dunlap, a division of Penguin Young Readers Group, 345 Hudson Street,
New York, New York 10014. ALL ABOARD READING and GROSSET & DUNLAP are trademarks
of Penguin Group (USA) Inc. Published simultaneously in Canada. Printed in the U.S.A.

Library of Congress Cataloging-in-Publication Data

Dubowski, Cathy East.
  Snug Bug / by Cathy East Dubowski and Mark Dubowski.
    p.   cm. — (All aboard reading)
  Summary: Relates the bedtime activities of a little bug in a big house.
  [1. Bedtime—Fiction.   2. Insects—Fiction.   3. Stories in rhyme.]   I. Dubowski, Mark, ill.
II. Title. III. Series.
PZ8.3.D8525Sn   1995
[E]—dc20   94-22489
                                                                               CIP
ISBN 978-0-448-40849-1   21 22 23 24 25 26 27 28 29   AC

Snug Bug

By Cathy East Dubowski
and Mark Dubowski

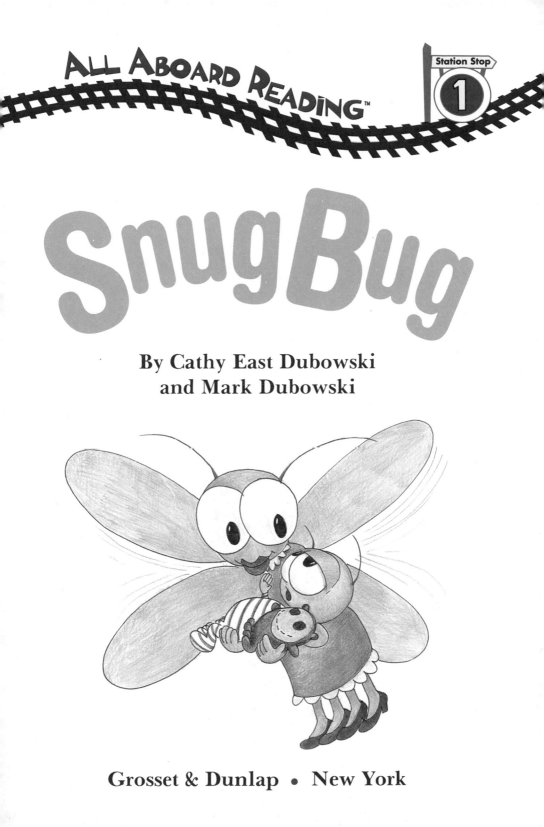

Grosset & Dunlap • New York

"It's time for the tub.
Put your toys away."

But Snug Bug says,
"I want to play."

"Where have you gone?"
asks Mama Bug.
Snug Bug is hiding.
(He's under the rug!)

Mama Bug knows.

She tugs at the rug.

"There you are,
   my little Snug Bug!"

Into the tub.

Scrub,

scrub,

scrub.

"Wheee!

Look at me!"

Mama Bug says,

"Your bath is done."

Snug Bug says,

"But I'm having fun!"

Glub,

      glub,

           glub.

Rub,

      rub,

           rub.

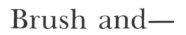

Brush and—

spit!

That's it!

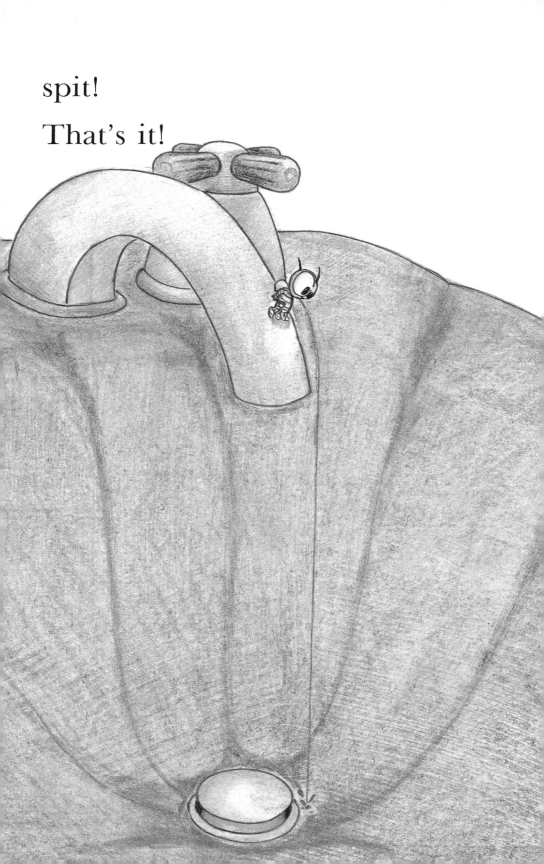

Now it's time to look
for a go-to-bed book.

Little Miss Muffet
sat on a tuffet . . .

Snug Bug knows
the rest by heart.
"The spider is
my favorite part!"

It's time for bed.

Is Snug Bug ready?

No!

He says,

"Where's my teddy?"

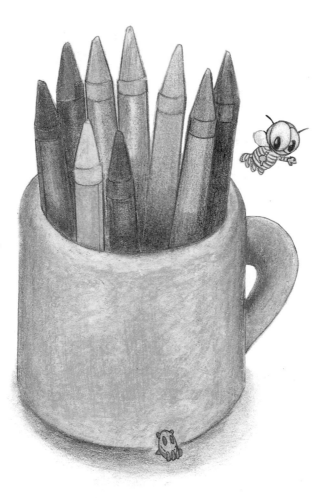

Snug Bug looks
behind the mug.
"There you are,
Teddy Bug!"

Mama Bug says,
"Now into bed."
Snug Bug nods
his sleepy head.

"Sweet dreams, Snug Bug,"
says Mama Bug.
She gives Snug Bug
a big buggy hug.

"Mama!" cries Snug Bug.

"Come back! Help! Hurry!

There's something here…

…It's big and furry!"

Mama comes back.
She hears his cries.
"It's only a boy.
Just shut your eyes."

Snug Bug smiles.

Mama tucks him back in.

She pulls the covers
up to his chin.

Now they are sleeping,
boy and bug—

snug

as a bug

in a rug.